My Dog Too

©2013 Dana Landers

Prologue

She would definitely have to be more careful going out during the day. If someone saw her, it would ruin everything. But she had been so hungry, and the small apple tree laden with unpicked fruit had been too hard to resist. Since it was just barely past dawn, she was pretty sure no one would have seen her. She settled herself back into a corner of the loft where there was a good view of the farmhouse through a crack in the old boards of the barn. When she had come across the unoccupied farm two days ago, she had decided the old barn was the perfect place to hide for a few days while she made her plan. But there was a family living here now and that changed everything.

Emma figured that the people who now lived in the house must be the new owners. She had secretly watched as two men unloaded boxes and furniture from a small moving van the day before and there was now a stack of broken-down boxes sitting to one side of the porch.   All day yesterday Emma had stayed quiet and hidden while the commotion of moving took place. She was so afraid that the movers would be bringing items to store in the old barn. But everything had been unloaded into the house and the garage, so she felt secure and safe in her little hideout. In the few chances she took to watch the goings on, she had seen a little girl a few years younger than herself, and a brown scruffy mutt that seemed to be glued to her side everywhere she went. There had been a man and a woman as well, but Emma had only had glimpses of them as they went from the truck to the house. Today would be for watching, waiting and learning more about this new family.

Chapter 1

It was an unusually warm day for the end of October, and everyone was taking advantage of it, knowing that the first snowfall could arrive at any time. This was probably the only time of the year that wasn't really spectacular in Lilac Creek. The blaze of fall color was gone, and the dazzling white of winter had not yet arrived. The fragrance and purple haze of spring lilacs were a distant memory, as were the lush green woodlands and sparkling blue waters of summer.   This was what Julia often called the "grey" season.

 But in today's unusually warm sun, she sat on the front porch absently rubbing the melon that was now her belly, reflecting on how much her life had changed in the past two years. Back then, her world revolved around her work, with what spare time she did have going to renovations on the house. Now here she was, seven months pregnant, watching her five-year-old daughter playing in the yard with her husband Sam, and their adopted dog Jasper! Julia was still amazed at how quickly she had grown to love the big brown mutt that had come so unexpectedly into her life. And becoming a wife and mother had been the icing on the cake. Yes, life was good, indeed, but even more changes were in store, one of the biggest ones being their move to the farm. Tomorrow they would move from their cozy little duplex to the big old farmhouse previously owned by Henry Thompson, Jasper's original owner.

Since he was living permanently at the long-term care centre, his daughter Wendy had decided it was time to sell his farm. She had naturally contacted Julia, Lilac Creek's main realtor. Julia had taken several trips out to the property and she and Sam had gone through the old house thoroughly in preparation for listing it on the market. On one of those trips, it suddenly hit Julia that this could be just the place for her growing family. They had been discussing moving to a bigger place for some time but nothing that really struck them had come onto the market lately. It was well into fall and not a time when most folks wanted to move, since school had already begun for the new term.

But as Julia wandered through the house on one particular visit, everything just seemed to click into place. There were four bedrooms upstairs, a big open kitchen and a large living room dining room combination on the main level. Another couple of rooms off the living room would serve nicely as a family room and an office, so Julia could work from home once the baby arrived. She and Sam had discussed it at length and when they asked Brinn for her opinion, she was over the moon with excitement. Living on a farm seemed to her to be about the best idea in the world, and the fact that Jasper would be moving back to his original home made it seem just perfect. And now, their cozy little house was almost all packed up and ready for the move.

After a while, Sam, Brinn and Jasper joined her on the porch for a rest. Jasper might be getting on in years, but his energy level was quite incredible. Both Sam and Brinn were still trying to catch their breath. "I swear that dog could run all day!" sighed Sam as he fell into the chair beside Julia. Brinn was sprawled on the porch beside Jasper, nose to nose, one arm around his scruff as she had always done from the first day they met. Julia was certain the dog could read Brinn's mind, they were so in tune with each other. She marveled at the changes that the last two years had meant for Brinn. She had gone from a traumatized preschooler who wouldn't speak, to a thriving five-year-old with a contagious love for life that rubbed off on everyone she met. Her adopted dog Jasper had been the catalyst for that remarkable recovery and Julia thanked her lucky stars every day for his constant devotion. Jasper had changed all of their lives in so many ways.

Once they had rested a bit, Sam suggested that they head inside to wash up and get changed. "Since the kitchen is all packed up and the movers are coming early in the morning, how about I take my favorite ladies out for supper?" When Jasper woofed, everyone laughed, and Sam agreed that his favorite furry gentleman could come too. "I know you think you're a person," Sam laughed as he rubbed Jasper's head, but you'll have to wait in the car, I'm afraid!" As if he understood, Jasper began spinning in circles and barking. He didn't care what he had to do as long as he got to go along.

Chapter 2

Brinn was so excited she could barely sit still. She was sitting in the middle of the living room floor surrounded by boxes and furniture, throwing a tennis ball for Jasper down the empty space in the middle of the room. As usual Jasper was running full tilt after the ball with little consideration for the fact that all of the rugs had been rolled up and the hardwood floors were like a big skating rink. Each time he tried to run he did an award-winning imitation of Bambi first discovering ice. But it didn't slow him down. Each time he would scramble till his feet found purchase and then slide into the wall at the other end to capture his prize.   As comical as the routine was, Brinn hardly noticed. All she could think about was getting out to the farm and discovering all the great new adventures just waiting for her there.

This was the first move that she was really old enough to be excited about. She had been too young to remember their move to Lilac Creek. All she really remembered from that move was an overwhelming sense of sadness because Mommy wasn't coming with them. At first, unable to accept the reality of losing her Mom, she remained silent and steadfast in her belief that her Mom had simply stayed behind at their old house, and that she would join them soon. Eventually, the love and patience of a devoted father helped her remember just why her Mom was not with them, and to accept their new situation. For a long time, she was unable to talk about it, but Jasper had changed all that. He had become her loving protector and faithful companion, helping her become once again the cheerful little girl she had been before. And now they were going to live in the house where Jasper used to live and to Brinn that was like a miracle. Brinn tossed the tennis ball once again down their makeshift alleyway, but instead of going after it, Jasper ran in the completely opposite direction barking wildly.

"The movers are here!" Brinn
shouted, jumping up to follow
behind the crazed Jasper. "Yay! It's
time to go!" Brinn followed Jasper
to the window where they could
watch what was going on but not be
in the way. Brinn could see her
Mom and Dad talking to the moving
men as they opened the huge back
door of the truck. She continued to
watch with amazement as they
unfolded a long ramp that extended
from the back of the truck, across
the porch stairs and right up to the
front door. It looked like a little
bridge and Brinn thought it would
be lots of fun to play on. But she
knew she was supposed to stay out
of the way, so she had to be
content with just watching.

Once the truck and ramp were in place, the movers and her parents came inside to plan out the loading of the truck. Always his jovial friendly self, Jasper circled their legs and wagged his bushy tail as if they were his long-lost friends. Each of the movers scratched his ears just as he was hoping they would and then continued with the task at hand. When Sam and the movers headed upstairs so they could see what they had to pack from those rooms, Julia called Brinn and Jasper into the kitchen. "I need you to pack up the bag of toys that you kept out for today, along with Jasper's things, "she said. "We're going to head out to the farm now so we can get things opened up and ready for the movers when they arrive."

"Okay," replied Brinn without hesitation. She was ready to get out to the farm and start exploring the new surroundings. She quickly threw all of her things into her backpack and stuffed Jasper's tennis balls, dishes, chew toys and blanket into another bag. She met her Mom at the car and climbed into her booster seat in the back. Jasper hopped in beside her, curling his big body as best he could to fit the confined space. Julia placed a few last items that they had used for breakfast into the trunk and slammed it closed.

As she started to back down the driveway, the full impact of leaving the very first home she had bought suddenly hit her. She had spent hours and hours on all the renovations and landscaping, and every single one of those undertakings was a labor of love. She had turned the rather run-down property into a cozy welcoming home, one that she had shared with an amazing man who had first been a kind, caring neighbor, and who was now her husband.

When she looked at the garden, she could picture Brinn sitting there playing, silent and sad in her grief, until Jasper licked her face one day and turned her whole upside-down world back right again. She thought back on the small wedding ceremony they had held right there in this same garden with just a few close friends and family. She could almost smell the lilacs that were in full bloom, and she could see Brinn walking down the path in her lavender dress, Jasper at her side, a big purple bow around his neck. Jasper had been the perfect gentleman, sitting proud and still beside his little girl all through the ceremony. She smiled then, remembering what had finally made him come undone. Just as the minister introduced them as the new Mr. and Mrs. Sam Baxter, a small red squirrel had run across the top of the garden fence right under Jasper's nose. He had taken off in hot pursuit, through the gate and out into the garden. No harm was done, and everyone agreed that he had already surpassed all expectations of good dog behavior and cheered him on. The squirrel eventually disappeared up an old oak tree and out of sight. Jasper returned to the group with a "mission accomplished" grin on his furry face.

Julia was completely swamped by the flood of memories that just kept coming. Only the insistent voice in the back seat brought her back into the realm of reality. "Mommy! Are we going now?" Judging by her tone, Julia figured Brinn had probably asked her a number of times already.

"Yes, love, we're going now." Julia started the car moving again. She and Sam would come back tomorrow for a final walkthrough of the duplex. She would say her final goodbyes then. Happy to be on the move finally, Brinn settled in to talk to Jasper about the excitement that lay ahead. She told him all about how he was going back to the farm where he used to live, and how they were going to fix it all up and make it their own house. Busy with her conversation, she was occupied for the whole trip out to the farm.

As they approached the turnoff to the country road leading to the farm, Jasper began to get very restless. He started to whine and yip in the back seat, standing up to look out the window as they drove. The big bushy tail started to wave back and forth and had Brinn not been in the seat beside him, Julia is certain he would have started pacing back and forth from window to window. The whining turned into a full-fledged bark when they turned into the long laneway leading to the house. "I think he recognizes this place, "Julia said to Brinn who was concerned by Jasper's erratic behavior. "He remembers that this is where he used to live." It was all they could do to keep Jasper from climbing over top of Brinn to get out once they stopped the car. A stern "Wait!" from Julia calmed him down while she got Brinn safely out of his way. Once he got the go-ahead signal, he bounded out of the back seat and started running frantically around the yard. He ran and sniffed every corner of the garden and then stood anxiously by the door waiting for Julia to undo the lock. As she pushed the door open, Jasper bolted inside running from room to room, nose sniffing and tail wagging. Brinn was jumping up and down and following him all around, completely caught up in the excitement. But Julia saw his excitement for what it really was, and her heart went out to the furry mutt.

Before long the frantic sniffing from room to room slowed down, and the excited bark became more of a whimper. Having sniffed out every corner of the house, he turned his big brown eyes to Julia, and she could see the question there.

"Where is he?" Julia was certain he was asking. "I thought Henry would be here," he seemed to be saying. Julia bent down to ruffle his long fur.

 "I know, Bud," she said softly. "You thought he would be here didn't you?" In all the excitement over moving, she hadn't even thought about this maybe happening, that Jasper would expect the old man to be there. How was a dog supposed to remember that the man who had loved him and raised him for so many years wasn't there anymore? Jasper had just blended into their lives so easily that they sometimes forgot he hadn't been theirs forever. Julia continued to stroke the furry head and show him as much love as she could. She knew in time, Jasper would accept that while this was the house where he and Henry had lived, that Henry himself was no longer there. Julia made a mental note to take Jasper for a visit to see Henry at the hospital as soon as they got settled in. In the meantime, there was a lot of work to be done to get to that point. Thinking that Jasper was likely responding to her feelings as much as anything else, Julia changed her tone and offered Jasper one of the treats from his bag. He responded readily and the next thing she knew he and Brinn were off looking for secret hideaways that somehow Brinn had convinced herself came with the house.

Sam and the movers arrived a few hours later and the rest of the day was spent getting everything moved into the house. A chilly October rain had begun to fall so they tried to hurry things along. Once the moving van was unloaded, the big truck pulled away and the family was left on their own. Brinn was disappointed that the rain kept them from doing much exploring outside, but she and Jasper ran from empty room to empty room imagining all the many ways they were going to enjoy their new space. Before long, night had fallen, and the darkness of the country property felt strange and a little bit scary to Brinn. They lit a warm fire in the fireplace and gathered around it, exhausted from the long day. Jasper and Brinn

curled up together on a big blanket
in front of the fire and quickly fell
asleep.

Chapter 3

Emma knew the people in the house were up and about now because soft light filtered through the lacy curtains. She could hear sounds of someone clanking dishes in the kitchen, but she was too far away to hear any voices. Suddenly someone opened the screen door and the big brown and black dog she had seen yesterday came bounding out, ready for play after his night inside. The dog was about the size of the golden retriever she remembered from her last school where he was a guide dog for a little blind girl. This dog wasn't golden at all though, but mostly brown with some black and tan on

his legs and haunches. He had a
big scruffy collar and ears that
looked as though they couldn't
decide whether to stand up or fall
down. He appeared to have a
perpetual smile on his face as he
charged about, his tail waving like a
banner as he ran. Emma wanted
so badly to go and run with him,
have him jump beside her as he
waited impatiently for her to throw a
stick. She wanted nothing more
than to run through this meadow
with that dog at her heels
discovering all kinds of treasures
along the way. He continued to race
about for a while and then settled
down to the serious business of
sniffing around. Nose to the
ground, he became intent on
identifying every creature that had

passed through the property the night before.

Suddenly Emma froze. What if he could smell her? What if he stood at the door to the old barn and started barking to alert the new owners to a stranger in the loft? Emma remembered reading once about how powerful a dog's sense of smell was, and that they could tell everything about a friend or foe by sniffing where they had been. Instinctively, Emma pulled herself into a ball and stayed very still. She scrunched her eyes closed and willed the dog to go away. After a time, he did just that. Emma allowed herself to breathe normally again but she remained absolutely still. Staying out of sight of people was one thing, but avoiding a big, curious dog was quite another matter.

After a time, the screen door opened again, and a woman appeared with a large stainless-steel bowl. She sat the bowl down in a corner of the porch and within seconds the dog came running from clear across the yard to devour its contents. Emma smiled along with the woman who gave the dog's ears a scratch before turning around and heading inside. Emma thought she looked like a really nice, happy lady. Her hair was pulled back in a ponytail that poked through the back of a faded blue ball cap, and her oversized gray sweatshirt said "Big Dog" in bold letters across the front. From her secret spot in the loft, Emma watched the proceedings with a big smile on her face and a deep sense of longing in her heart. She didn't know why, but something inside told her this lady was a person she would like to have as a friend. As she walked away the lady waved a finger lovingly at the big mutt. "Now don't gobble!" she said laughingly. Emma remembered how her dog Tucker had always gobbled down his food like it was the last meal he was ever going to have. She remembered how her mother used to say "Now, Tucker, don't gobble." It never mattered. Tucker gobbled every time. But that was a long time ago. Emma felt that old familiar tug in her heart.

She had only been four the last time she and her parents had been together, but she had deep rooted memories of those happy times. Her parents, their cabin and Tucker had been her whole world. Neither of her parents had any other family and there were no neighbors nearby. Her parents had chosen the small cabin at the edge of the woods for the solitude it would provide. Although the cabin had been small, Emma remembered it always being cozy and inviting. There was a large second cabin on the property that had served as a workplace for both her parents. It was just one big open space with a big stone fireplace that took up one entire wall. Her father had set up an office in one corner for his writing, and her mom had claimed the rest of the space as a studio where she created magnificent paintings. Emma could remember spending her days playing on the rug in front of the fire. She and Tucker would play there for hours while her parents worked. There was a big basket of toys on each side of the fireplace, one for her and one for Tucker. He would lie beside her chewing one of his squeaky toys while she played with her dolls or her stuffed animals. Somehow, he would always sense when she was growing bored with what she was doing, and right then he would get up and dig through his toy basket for a ball or a stick. He would bring it over to her and drop it in her lap as much as to say, "Ok, now it's time to play." Emma would get her outdoor clothes on and out they'd go. Her Mom would always have a snack ready for her when they came back in.

 She closed her eyes as she sat in the old deserted loft and remembered those happy days. But things were different now. In one split second her happy world had been shattered and everything she held dear had been taken from her. Now she was on her own, completely alone, but thankful for her treasured memories and this deserted barn that for now would provide her with the shelter she needed and the freedom she so desperately wanted.

At last, with his belly full and his morning routines completed, the big dog flopped onto the wooden floor of the porch, claiming a big sun-drenched space for his very own. Emma's fingers almost itched with a desire to bury her face in the silky fur and breathe in that soothing aroma of warm dog.

But Emma knew she had to stay hidden. No matter how nice that lady might seem, if she found Emma hiding in her barn, she would have to go back to another foster home. Emma just didn't think she could stand that again.

She was so confused. She didn't really know where she planned to go, but something in her heart kept pulling her towards her old home.

Although sensibility tried to niggle its way to the front of her thinking, Emma squashed it down and told herself that if she could just make it back to their old cabin, she could be happy. Maybe, she thought, no one had moved into their cabin. Maybe, even if someone had, there was a chance they wouldn't be using the workshop. She could set up a little home for herself there. And in weaving her web of dreams, she imagined that maybe Tucker was still living there too. No one had ever told her what really happened to Tucker when they came to take her away from her home. All the lady who picked her up said was that he would be taken care of.

At the time, there was nothing Emma could do but go along. Her parents were gone, she had to go live with strangers, and she never saw Tucker again. In her fantasy, Tucker would be there waiting for her when she finally made her way home. They would hide out together in the cozy workshop and be happy forever. All she had to do was get there.

But for now, she had to concentrate on staying hidden while she made her plan. She scooted back into the shadows of the barn's loft and settled herself into the little bed that she had made by scraping some loose straw together into a pile. She could hear voices coming from the farmhouse, but she didn't want to risk moving around in case they headed her way.

After a time, she also heard doors slamming and car engines starting. Knowing that they were all near the driveway, Emma chanced a glimpse out the little crack that served as her window on the world. The nice lady was leaving in the little car, and the man, the dog and the little girl were all in the truck. Emma was surprised at the sudden feeling of loneliness that came over her at the thought that they were all leaving. She had been comforted knowing they were around even though they were totally unaware of her presence.

After a few minutes, though, she realized that maybe this would be the perfect opportunity to sneak inside and borrow a few supplies for her journey, and some food for her rumbling belly. She really hoped that the door wouldn't be locked. She felt a little pang of guilt as she contemplated taking things that weren't hers for the taking, but she really only needed a little food and maybe another warm blanket or two.

Emma waited for a few minutes to make sure both car and truck were not coming back for some reason, and then she scooted over to the rickety old ladder and climbed carefully down. She crouched low as she made her way across the lawn to the house even though she knew the people inside were gone.

It was almost a habit now, to stay low and stay quiet. She moved quickly, not wanting to chance being out in the open if someone came by. She crossed the wide plank floor of the porch and held her breath as she turned the old wobbly doorknob. The door was a bit sticky, but it wasn't locked, and it pushed open with a creak and a groan. Emma left the door standing open as she slowly entered the mud room off the kitchen. There were still boxes piled everywhere and she had to weave her way through them. She finally came into the bright sunlit kitchen. The paint was faded but a bright checkered cloth adorned the round table and a big bowl of fruit in the middle made her mouth start to water. She peeked into the fridge and helped herself to two bottles of water from the dozen or so that were there. She really didn't think anyone would miss them. She added a container of yogurt and a bagel to the water and sat everything on the table beside the fruit bowl then went to continue her search for something to help her stay warm at night. There was a big fluffy blanket on the floor in front of the fireplace, but Emma knew that taking it would be too obvious. Instead, she retreated back to the mud room where she had seen several old wooden shelves loaded with all kinds of stuff. From the haphazard way things were piled on the shelves and the dust that had settled on most of them, Emma decided that they must be things left behind by the previous owners. If that was the case, she figured the new owners wouldn't even know she had taken anything. She quickly scanned the items and was excited to find an old flannel sleeping bag rolled up in one corner. She pulled it down and undid the straps. The long tube of sleeping bag would work as a sack to carry her supplies back to the loft. She quickly stuffed a second blanket and an old knitted sweater into the makeshift bag and headed back to the kitchen. There, she put the two water bottles, yogurt and bagel into the bag along with an apple and an orange. She really wanted the banana that was there too, but there was only one and she thought someone might notice if it was gone. Hoisting the sack over her shoulder, Emma took one last quick look around the mud room. She would love to have some warmer boots and socks, but it didn't seem like there was anything like that around. She decided that what she had found on this trip would do for now, and she was starting to get a little nervous about being in the house so long. She pulled the old creaky door shut behind her as she headed back to her little safe haven in the loft, her mind happy with the thought of some yummy snacks and a warmer night's sleep.

Chapter 4

In town, Julia quickly finished up her errands. She wanted to get back to the farm and get some more unpacking and organizing done. Sam had taken Brinn and Jasper to the playground to give her a bit of time to work without any distractions. They would only be gone a while and Julia really hoped that would give her time to at least get the kitchen unpacked. The trip into town had already eaten up some of that time but she had desperately needed some cleaning supplies and storage bins to do justice to the long-neglected kitchen cupboards. So, it was with some impatience that she answered the greeting from an acquaintance as she left the grocery store.

"Julia! Nice to see you." The voice came from the car two spaces over. It was Carol Lindstrom. Carol was well known in Lilac Creek as "The Foster Mom" to several kids of varying ages. Julia didn't know her well but had met one little girl in her care who was a friend of Brinn's. They had exchanged pleasantries at several birthday parties and soccer games.

"Oh, hi, Carol," Julia said, shoving a very huge bag of dog kibble into the very small trunk of her car. "Shopping for all those hungry mouths you have to feed?"

"As always!" answered Carol with a small smile and a shrug. "But have you heard the latest? We have one less mouth to feed right now."

"No, I hadn't heard," said Julia as she slammed the trunk closed. "Did one of your kids go back home?"

"I wish it were that simple! No, our most recent and most short staying member, Emma, just up and ran away. The Sherriff has been by and everyone's looking for her, but no news yet. Greg and I feel just awful."

"Don't be too hard on yourself," Julia offered supportively. "You know better than anyone how these kids can just get an idea in their head and run with it. No doubt she'll turn up at a friends' house or the local drop in centre."

"Ya, I hope you're right," Carol said and shrugged again. "Anyway, keep your eyes peeled for a brown haired, brown eyed dynamo about four and half feet tall. She's a real firecracker and not the least bit afraid of being on her own. If she has decided to head out of town she might very well wander by your new place. How is the move going by the way?"

"We're getting there, slowly but surely," Julia replied thinking to herself how fast news travels in a small town like Lilac Creek.

"I'll keep an eye out for Emma," Julia assured her, wondering what would make a ten year old little girl prefer to be on her own instead of in the care of a couple who seemed as caring as Carol and Greg.   Just the thought of a lonely little girl out in the world all alone made her remember how sad Brinn had been when they first met. But not anymore. Jasper had changed all of that. Julia imagined for a moment that maybe, if Emma did happen by their new place, that one big slobbery kiss from Jasper could be just the thing to help her too!

Julia's imagination started painting a picture of Brinn and an older sister running through the fields around the old farm with a barking Jasper leading the way.   She herself would be sitting on the big verandah in a creaky wooden rocker watching them play as she cradled their new little baby in her arms. Eventually they would all congregate on the porch for cold drinks and snacks, each one, including the dog, taking turns kissing those chubby baby cheeks.

Julia couldn't help but laugh at herself and her vivid imagination. Giving her head a little shake, she returned to her thoughts of cupboard cleaning and unpacking. Armed with all her supplies, Julia headed for home. It still amazed her every time she made the trip to and from town that they now owned a big old house in the country! When she had bought the duplex in town, she was certain that she would never leave, or ever be able to love another house as much as she loved that place. But life really has a way of upsetting the apple cart! Now here she was married to a fantastic man with a five year old daughter and another baby on the way, all because her car one wintery day decided to collide with a big brown and tan mutt named Jasper. As if on cue, Jasper came running down the lane at the sound of her car approaching.

"Well I guess I didn't beat them home," thought Julia to herself and smiling at the fur ball flying towards her. She slowed the car to a crawl so she could keep an eye on him and pulled carefully into her parking spot. Jasper was still barking, and his ruckus had Brinn and Sam both coming out of the house to see what was going on.

"No fear of arriving unnoticed is there?" she directed at Sam.

"Not a chance!" he laughed as he started helping her unload the bags in the back seat. "If you were hoping for an element of surprise, you were definitely barking up the wrong tree! Pardon the pun, I couldn't resist!" They both laughed and headed for the house, watching Jasper change his focus immediately to Brinn when he saw her come out of the house.

"Can I stay outside with Jasper?" asked Brinn." We'll just play in the meadow." Julia looked to Sam who glanced around the wide expanse of yard bordered by the much thicker brush and forest.

"You can play here in the open areas," said Sam as he gestured to the grassy area between the house and the old barn. "Don't go into the woods or behind the barn. Stay where your Mom and I can see you from the house, ok?"

"Ok," replied Brinn. She loved being outside and to her the whole world was full of possibilities of adventure. With Jasper at her side, they were an invincible pair and without a bit of direction, they would go anywhere, try anything. They headed happily off to investigate the abandoned vegetable garden where her Mom had said they might find some carrots or squash still good for eating. After pulling up a few remaining carrots from the garden, Brinn quickly became distracted by the little stream that flowed past the garden in behind the old barn and off into the woods. The water was crystal clear, and Jasper didn't hesitate to jump in. Because she hadn't thought to put her rubber boots on, Brinn remained on shore, laughing as Jasper tried to unearth big rocks from the bottom of the stream. He would find one that he liked, dig at it for a while and then dive his nose in to try and remove it. He didn't really like having his head under the water, though, so he would come up snorting and snuffling with water flying everywhere as he shook. Then he'd take a couple breaths and repeat the whole act all over again, each time with lots of yipping and yapping. Brinn laughed at his antics and cheered him on. "Isn't this fun, Jasper?" she squealed. "I knew we would have tons of adventures here on the farm!" When they tired of that game, Brinn found a big gnarled stick and started tossing it for Jasper to catch. Giving it all she had, Brinn threw the stick out into the open meadow. Several times Jasper chased it and brought it back. Then he got distracted by a flock of geese flying overhead and wasn't looking when Brinn made a long and hard throw in the direction of the old barn. When Jasper turned to her again the stick was already long gone and he had no idea which direction to go. Looking at her with a big goofy dog expression, Jasper just stood there waiting. "Well come on then," said Brinn. "We have to go find it." As she headed out into the meadow Jasper barked his approval.

The sound of a dog barking very nearby roused Emma from her daydreams. She stole a quick peek through the cracks in the siding of the barn. She could see the little girl and the dog moving closer as they played in the stream. Her heart started to race and she could feel it pounding in her ears. What if the dog smelled her? What if they came into the barn and found her? Emma held her breath and stayed very still. She was holding all her muscles so tight they were starting to tremble. Now the little girl and the dog were right under the spot where Emma had been watching them. The little girl was laughing and talking to the dog as they passed by. "I threw it right over here! Didn't you watch where it went?" The dog barked loudly, and Emma held her breath. She was sure he had caught her scent and was trying to let the little girl know! But the girl simply ignored his barking as she kicked aside the long brown grass. After a few moments she bent down and retrieved the knobby old stick that the dog had been chasing. She waved it over her head, and teasingly called to the big dog. "Here it is Jasper! I found it!" At the sight of his refound treasure, the big dog began jumping up and barking

for the game to continue. The girl
threw the stick back towards the
house, and then continued to walk
in that direction herself. As the
distance between them and the
barn increased, Emma slowly
began to relax. She silently
released the breath she'd been
holding and crept up to peer
through the crack. The dog and his
little companion were now back at
the house. The little girl perched on
the porch steps while the dog took
a long drink from a big stainless-
steel bowl. When he was done, he
sprawled out at the girl's feet, ready
for the next round of play as soon
as she made the move. They spent
the remainder of the afternoon
alternating between exploratory
trips to the meadow and playing

hide and seek in the small orchard that grew off to one side of the property. The trees were small and had branches low to the ground just perfect for climbing, but Brinn wasn't quite tall enough to get all the way into the crook of the first branch. She settled instead, for picking a few of the last remaining apples to take home to her Mom. She had just picked the last of what she could carry when she heard her Mom calling her in for supper.

The days were getting a lot shorter now and the rest of her play time would have to be saved for indoors. But Brinn loved her new big room with the window that looked out over the meadow and she still had all her boxes of toys to unpack and

arrange on her shelves. She called
to Jasper and skipped all the way
back to the house, the big brown
dog never leaving her side.

Chapter 5

The nights were definitely starting to get colder and Emma was so glad that she had some warmer blankets and the warm sweater she had found. She so wished that she had a flashlight or some kind of lantern for the nighttime, but she hadn't been been able to find anything when she was in the house that morning. At times she could hear small rustling noises in other parts of the barn and she really wished she could see what was making them when they came too close. For the most part though, the old abandoned barn was quiet, relatively warm, and for now, at least, safe.

Through the long dark night Emma
dreamt that she was back at her
cabin feeding chocolate cake to
Tucker while her Mom and Dad sat
and chatted by the big fireplace. It
was a happy dream and the warm
feeling stayed with her as she
opened her eyes to a new day.
Then she remembered. She wasn't
at home. She wasn't even at the
Lindstrom's anymore. She was
here in this old abandoned barn, all
alone and only able to watch the
happy family who lived here from
her secret hiding place. She
couldn't even pet the awesome dog
that lived there. She couldn't take
the chance that she might be
discovered. The reality of being so
completely alone banished the
warm memories of her dream in an

instant. But Emma was not prone to feeling sorry for herself. Her Mom used to tell her that feeling sorry for yourself was nothing but a waste of time, and that if something was making you sad, then it was best to tackle it head on and look for a solution. So that was what Emma was going to do. Today she would start making plans for her future.

First, she would need to consider her options. Now that she had made the decision to run away, she wasn't really sure what her next step should be. All she could think about was getting back home, to be somewhere familiar, to maybe find some thread from her past that she could use to weave together a new life. But suddenly that option seemed so impossible. There would most likely be new people living in their cabin. Tucker was probably already happy in some new place and there wasn't anyone special from her old life that she could contact for help. So maybe that whole idea was a waste of time after all. She supposed that she could try to stay here and stay hidden in this old barn. If she were very careful, she could continue to sneak into the house for food and supplies. She could use the tiny stream that ran through the property to stay clean, and maybe she would even eventually make friends with the big dog without the family even finding out. She had all of the woods and meadows around the farm to explore when the family was gone for the day. If she was very, very careful, Emma thought, she could maybe even spend time indoors during their absence to watch a bit of television and maybe even cook some warm food for herself. She didn't really like the idea of stealing from the nice people, who lived here, but somehow it didn't really feel like stealing since she was only taking what she needed to survive, and she only took things that she thought they would never miss anyway.

As she let those plans roll around in her head, Emma started to feel pretty excited. Maybe this could work out after all! All she had to do was be really really careful and everything would be fine. Feeling almost happy for the first time in weeks, Emma took the pencil and notepad from her backpack and started making her list.

First on the list was another warm blanket. The nights were really starting to get cold. Second was maybe some warmer clothes if she could find something to fit. The lady who lived in the house was pretty tiny, and the little girl was only a bit smaller than she was, so that shouldn't be a problem. Some boots would be nice too, for doing her exploring. Emma hoped there would be an extra pair of rubber boots like those that always stayed on the mat outside the front door around somewhere that no one wore anymore. She remembered how her mom had always had extra boots in the storage room that she kept "just in case" after she bought new ones. Maybe, Emma thought, if I can find a storage room like that inside, I'll be able to find everything I need without anyone ever noticing.

For the rest of the day Emma busied herself with plans for making the old dusty loft her new home. She finished up the rest of the food she had found that morning and tidied up her sleeping bag and blankets in preparation for another night. It had been a rainy, chilly day and the family had spent the day inside. Occasionally the big dog came out into the yard, but even he was quick about his business and anxious to get back inside. The man had come out only briefly to let to gather wood from the porch. Emma could smell the smoke from a fireplace and though she wasn't curled up in front of it with people she loved, the smell alone helped warm her heart a little bit. She was quiet and careful whenever she needed to go out to use her makeshift "bathroom." She had cleared away some of the grass form a little spot behind some bushes where she was well hidden from the house. It wasn't really fun having to "go" outside, but Emma used her imagination to help make it easier. Sometimes she would pretend she was on a big outdoor adventure, or sometimes she would pretend she was a little girl back in pioneer days when they didn't have indoor bathrooms. Emma had loved watching old episodes of Little House on the Prairie and often imagined what it would have been like to be Laura Ingalls. With those thoughts on her mind, Emma pulled out her pencil once again and added toilet paper to her list of supplies.

When night again fell in earnest, Emma was both comforted and disturbed by the darkness. She knew she was safe from being found so she could relax about that, but the total darkness and silence made her more than a little bit lonely. She pulled on the warm sweater and curled up in her new sleeping bag, tucking the stuffed dog she always carried with her under her head for a pillow.

Inside the farmhouse, quite cozy in her new room, Brinn looked out over the dark meadow towards the big bulk of the old barn that stood outlined in the moonlight. "Maybe we'll get to explore that tomorrow if it stops raining," she whispered into Jasper's ear as she hugged him goodnight. Jasper licked her hand and did his usual round of spins before flopping down on his big foam bed.

Chapter 6

"Good morning sunshine," Sam said as he tousled Brinn's hair. "How was your first night in your new room? Sleep okay?

Brinn nodded her mouth full of the fresh apple muffins that Julia had just baked that morning. "I was a little scared of the dark at first, but Jasper slept right by my bed all night!"

"What big plans do you and Jasper have for today?" Sam asked as he finished pouring his coffee and brought it to the table, stopping to give Jasper a scratch on the way.

"We're going to explore some more, "replied Brinn with all of her usual enthusiasm. "Can me and Jasper look around in the old barn today?"

"Jasper and I," corrected Julia as she walked into the kitchen, and "I'm not sure if that would be a good idea. It's pretty run down and could be unsafe." Julia looked to Sam.

"I think it would be okay as long as you're really careful and promise not to be too much of a daredevil. Just have a look around but don't touch stuff or climb up those old stairs to the loft."

"I won't "promised Brinn with all her typical five year old confidence. "We'll be really careful. I just want to see what it's like inside. Come on, Jasper, let's get ready!" Brinn ran upstairs to get dressed and ready for another day of adventure, Jasper at her heels.

Out in the loft, another young girl was also getting ready to face the day. Emma had been out already to her little spot behind the barn. She had washed up a bit in the stream, but the water was getting really cold and it wasn't very much fun. She quickly ran back into the barn and up to the loft, pulling the blankets around her once again just to get warm. Just as she got settled, she heard the screen door of the porch slam, followed instantly by barking and the happy singing of the little girl. Cuddled in her blanket cocoon, Emma didn't move to the window to see what they were doing. She assumed the girl and dog would be hunting for rabbits or digging for vegetables or playing a game of fetch as they had done the day before. It wasn't until she heard the creak of the barn door that she realized they were coming into the barn. Emma froze. There was nothing she could do but stay as still as she could and hope they didn't climb the ladder to the loft.

Spooked a little by the dark dusty interior of the barn, Brinn wandered around the almost empty space whispering her thoughts to Jasper. "This place is kind of creepy," she said, keeping one hand on Jasper's scruff. She took in the big open space, the few old wooden crates stacked against one wall, and the rickety looking ladder that led to the loft. A concerned barn swallow that heard her come in swooped above her head before perching on one of the high rafters. Brinn gave a little screech at the sudden movement, and Jasper barked, making her jump again. When she realized it was nothing but a bird, Brinn laughed and plopped herself down on the bottom step of the ladder. "That was scary," she said out loud to Jasper, and then she laughed. "Some explorers we are, getting scared by a little bird!" Jasper barked in agreement.

Suddenly Jasper's nose went straight up in the air and he began taking big sniffs of the musty barn air. Next he started to bark and pace all around the bottom of the ladder. "It's ok, Jasper" Brinn reassured him. "It was just a bird." When Jasper refused to stop barking, Brinn's heart started to beat faster and she got a little scared. Jasper just kept barking and pacing and looking up into the loft. Brinn jumped up off the bottom step of the ladder and tried to get a look into the loft. From where she stood, she could only see into a small portion of the loft, but as far as she could tell, the space was empty. There was no sound coming from the loft and Brinn wondered what Jasper was getting all excited about. He had stopped barking now and stood resting his front paws on the bottom step where Brinn had been sitting. He was looking directly into the loft now, bushy tail wagging and his occasional short bark changing almost to a whimper from time to time. Brinn was curious to know what he might think was up there, but she was also a bit creeped out. In her five year old imagination, even as brave as she was, thoughts of monsters and creatures and scary things loomed larger than life.

"Come on, Jasper," she coaxed. "I think we've done enough exploring in here for one day." She grabbed Jasper's collar and tried to move him toward the door. At first Jasper stood unmoving near the bottom of the ladder. "Jasper, come on!" Brinn pleaded. "I want to go home, now." At the change in his master's tone, Jasper looked away from the ladder, and still with some hesitation, followed her to the door.

Up in the loft, Emma breathed a sigh of relief when she heard the barn door creak closed. She started to realize just how hard it was going to be to stay hidden, especially now that the dog knew she was there. With a feeling of despair, Emma realized that having this family move into the old farmhouse had given her a false sense of security, almost as if she'd be able to live her secret life here, unnoticed and happy, supported just by their proximity. She was suddenly very sad and very confused. Maybe it was time to move on. As Emma sat and pondered what her next move should be, a plan started to form in her mind. If she could get into town, maybe she could find a warm place to hide out and make a home for herself. She had watched TV shows where kids had lived in old churches or schools all by themselves, getting handouts from store owners and people on the street. Maybe she would even find other runaway kids there to hide out with. All she had to do was get into town. She knew that the man had a pickup truck that he often took into town. If she could sneak up to the house and hide in the back of the truck, then she should be able to get into town. From there, she would search for another hiding place. Emma decided that for now, the best thing for her to do was to stay quiet, stay hidden, and try to figure out when to make her big move.

 It was hard keeping track of the days of the week when every day seemed the same, but she figured the man would probably go to his job most weekdays. Emma decided she would watch for a while and get to know his regular routine. It would have to be soon, though, because her supplies were running low and the old barn was getting pretty cold at night.

As the day wore on, Emma alternated between watching what was going on around the house and writing notes in her little book. She was afraid to venture out as long as the family was home, so the day was long and boring. At some point after she had eaten the last of the food that she had, she drifted off into a restless sleep. When she awoke again, the sun was setting behind the house. The days seemed really short now, and soon she would face another long, lonely night.

Chapter 7

Emma watched the smoke from the
chimney as it made a curling trail
into the sky. How she longed to sit
by the fire and soak up its warmth.
She was starting to think that
maybe leaving the Lindstrom's had
been a bad idea, for as unhappy
and lonely as she had been there,
at least she was warm and well fed.
She supposed another option would
be for her to turn herself in to the
family in the house and accept that
she might be returned to the
Lindstrom's or sent somewhere
else if they no longer wanted her.

It was a very lonely feeling to be
only ten years old and think that no
one wanted you. Emma felt the
tears well up in her eyes and slowly

trickle down her cheek. Her hand
was in mid air to wipe them away
when she heard the barn door
creak slowly open once again. She
instinctively lowered her hand to her
side and pulled herself silently into
a small ball. She listened so hard
for any sounds from below that she
thought her ear drums would pop.
She didn't hear any footsteps or
voices, just the slight creaking of
the door. Maybe the wind had just
blown it open. She waited silently
until she couldn't wait any longer,
and then she crept to the edge of
the ladder and peered down. Her
eyes were met by another pair of
equally brown, equally surprised
eyes set into a wide furry face with
a broad snout. Their eyes locked,
and for what seemed like forever to

Emma, neither dog nor girl moved. Then the bushy tail began to wag and the black line on the dog's muzzle seemed to curve up in a smile. When Emma finally tore her eyes away, she glanced behind the dog for the person she was certain would be there, but no one appeared.

The dog now had his paws resting on the bottom rung of the ladder almost implying that, if she didn't come down soon, he was coming up. Emma stood to a low crouch and edged her way toward the ladder, taking a quick look through the crack in the barn wall to see what was going on at the house. There was no sign of anyone outside, and the doors were all closed. Emma could make out some movement in the kitchen through the lacey curtain, but the windows were closed to the chilly fall air and she couldn't hear any voices. When she glanced down the ladder again, she was met with the same brown eyed gaze as before.

Now there seemed to be a question there. "Why won't you come down and see me?" the furry mutt seemed to say. "I just want to be your friend!" Emma smiled in spite of herself and finally couldn't resist. With one last glance behind the dog, she lowered herself onto the first step of the ladder. The closer she got, the faster the dog's tail wagged, and he began to prance in place, his nails clicking softly on the old wooden floor. Hoping with all her might that he wouldn't start barking, Emma jumped off the last step of the ladder and hugged the big scruffy neck. She buried her face in the wonderful woodsy smell of dog that she remembered from the old days. As if he understood her need for love, Jasper flopped to the floor and let this new little girl hug him just as he had allowed Brinn to do when they had first met. For Jasper, giving and receiving love was what made the world go round, with the odd game of fetch and a bowl of kibble thrown in for good measure. He stayed still until he felt her start to draw away.

"What are you doing out here all by yourself?" she asked. "And how did you get the door open?" Emma took another suspicious glance around as if asking the question would make someone appear. Maybe the little girl had left it unlatched earlier, she told herself, and this guy just happened to be out doing some necessary doggie business. If that was the case, someone would be calling for him soon, or even more likely, would come looking for him. Emma had to get the dog back outside and on his way home without getting herself discovered.

"Come on big guy," she whispered into Jasper's ear. "It's time for you to go home." She gave him one last hug and the pulled him towards the door by his collar. Stubborn as always, Jasper refused to budge. He knew this little girl needed his help, and she wasn't going to get it by his leaving her behind. Emma tugged and tugged on the collar, but the dog was too heavy for her to move without his cooperation.

"Please go home now," Emma pleaded. "You can't stay here. Please go back home." Desperate to be safe again, Emma went to the back of the dog and tried to push him forward toward the door. Meeting only more resistance, Emma couldn't help but start to cry. "You have to go. Now." She whispered tearfully. Jasper sensed her emotional upset and turned to

lick the tears from her cheeks.
Emma was so taken back by this
sudden show of compassion, that
she came completely undone.

All of the loneliness, fear and
uncertainty of the past few days
released itself as she slid to the
floor once again and sobbed into
the the warm fur under her hands.
She forgot to be careful. She forgot
to be quiet. She forgot everything
except how good it felt to let all her
feelings go. Jasper sat
uncomplaining in the same spot,
determined to help his new little
friend with the broken heart. Only
when he heard his other young
masters' voice calling from the back
porch did he stand to contemplate
leaving. Sensing his indecision,

Emma quickly pushed him towards the door, before she herself headed up the ladder to the loft. Jasper glanced back at the girl one last time as if to say, "I'll be back, don't you worry." And then he turned and went out into the early evening. Emma waited until she heard the screen door to house slam shut before she scurried down and quickly latched the old barn door.

Early the next morning Emma was awakened by the sounds of the old pickup truck pulling out of the drive. Not more than a few minutes later, Emma watched from the cracked wall of the barn as the little girl and the dog left with the woman in the small green car. Excited that this could be her chance to get into the house once again, Emma hurried down the steps, creating a cloud of dust as she jumped from the third step to the floor. She paused only briefly to have a quick look around before she headed towards the house.

The view down the road was blocked by the house from this angle, so she didn't see the yellow truck until it was all the way up the driveway. Emma's heart started beating wildly as she ducked behind the small shed that had been built near the vegetable garden for housing tools and gardening supplies. She heard the doors of the truck slam and the loud voices of two men reached her clearly. They were walking straight to the old barn. The combination of cold and fear had Emma shivering from head to toe. She had fled the barn so quickly, not wanting to waste any time getting what she needed from the house that she hadn't bothered to put on the warm sweater or her jacket. Now the cold seemed to be going right to her bones. She hugged her arms around herself as she crouched low behind the shed. She had no trouble making out the conversation that the two men were having.

"Guess this must be the one," said the larger of the two men. "It's the only barn I see around here."

"Yep," replied the other man. "Let's get inside and have a look around."

Emma stayed as still as she could
as she imagined the two men
discovering her little hiding place
and seeing all her belongings.
What would they think? What
would they do? Would they tell the
man who lived in the house that
someone was hiding in his barn?
Should she run away now before
they had a chance to find her? It
took all the resolve Emma had to
hold back the tears that threatened
to flow. I have to be quiet. I have
to be quiet. Emma repeated the
words like a mantra over and over
in her head.

Just when she thought her feet
would fall off from being so cold, the
two men emerged from the barn. It
was the big man's voice again that

she could hear. This time he was talking on a cell phone. He was telling someone that it was his recommendation that the old barn be torn down. There was nothing worth saving, in his opinion, and he could come back and finish the task in the next day or two. In the meantime, he recommended that they cut down the old stairs to the loft right away as they could pose a real risk to anybody who might try to use them. Thinking of Brinn, Sam agreed to the demolition and to the immediate removal of the old ladder. The big man disconnected and filled his partner in on the plan. "We're going to cut down the old ladder to the loft today and come back to finish the demolition of the whole barn, the day after tomorrow.

I'll head back to the truck for the gear and you take a quick look around the loft in case there's anything we should move down.

Emma couldn't believe her ears. They were going to find her things and they were going to cut down the ladder! And there wasn't one single thing she could do, except stay where she was until they were done and gone. Once they were both back inside the barn, Emma crept around the corner of the little shed and slipped inside. It was at least a little bit warmer in there, out of the wind, but there was barely enough room for her to fit. She crouched down in the corner and waited while the buzz of the chain

saw tore apart the only home she
had.

Chapter 8

Brinn opened the car door and jumped out, eager as always to greet the day. She absolutely loved being a big girl and going to school every day. She was a good student and the teachers often commented on her quick ability to absorb information. There didn't appear to be any delays caused by the entire year that she was unable to speak. The psychologists and teachers all agreed that even though she hadn't been speaking, the normal range of learning had still been taking place. She now chattered as much as any other five year old, and maybe even more. As she scrambled to gather her things from the seat of the car, Julia reminded her that her father would be picking her up at the end of the day. "I'm going over to Wilmot to visit for a bit with Henry. There are some things around the farm that he left there, and we need to know if he wants some of them. I won't be back in time to get you, but your Dad will be here."

"Are you taking Jasper with you?" Brinn asked.

"I am indeed," replied Julia. "Henry would never forgive me if I didn't!" Brinn laughed.

"Okay, Mom. Say hi to Henry for me. See you when you get home." Off she went, skipping her way to the door of the school. Julia waited until she was inside then drove away. Visiting hours at the hospital didn't start until one o'clock, so her plan was to spend the morning continuing with unpacking and organizing. She was anxious to get that part of the move over with so she could move on to decorating the nursery. Sam had already done the painting, but he was leaving the decorating up to her. Her doctor had told her that there was a possibility that she could go into labor early, and with only six weeks left until her due date, Julia wanted to have everything ready in plenty of time to spend the last week or so relaxing and preparing for the ordeal that she had heard that labor could be.

As they pulled into the driveway Jasper started getting fidgety. He was ready to get out of the car and get on about his doggie business. He usually stuck pretty close to home on days when Brinn was at school, but today he seemed particularly anxious to go exploring. As soon as Julia opened the car door, he was off and running. He stopped briefly along the edge of the drive to relieve himself, and then took off towards the old barn. He had his nose to the ground like a hound on the hunt. Julia smiled to herself. Sam had just texted her to say that the men had been to the house to inspect the old barn, and she was pretty sure that their scent was probably lingering around, giving Jasper good cause to be suspicious. She watched him for a few minutes until she was sure he wasn't going to go far, and then she headed on into the house.

Meanwhile, Jasper continued to sniff all around the perimeter of the barn. He could smell the men who had been there, but he could also smell the new acquaintance he had made the other day. He followed her scent to the little shed by the garden and then back again to the barn. He sensed that she was upset and in need of comfort. He started to whine softly in hopes that she might hear him and open the creaky old door so he could warm her with his furry coat and comfort her with some cold nosed kisses. Inside, Emma could hear the dog at the door. She was so distraught by what she had found when she returned to the barn, that she didn't even hesitate to let him in. She opened the door just a crack and Jasper slithered through the small opening. Emma sank to the dusty floor right there beside him and let her lonely tears fall on the soft fur. Starved for personal contact, she hugged him close and let all her feelings pour out. She told him all about the men who had been at the barn and how they had moved her things out of the loft and put them in an old crate. She sobbed as she told him that the old barn was going to be torn down, so that now, without a hiding place, she would have to leave right away or risk being found. "I don't know what to do," she cried into the floppy brown ears. "I just want a home, and a family and someone who wants me." As if he understood, Jasper started licking the tears from her cheeks. "I wish you could be my dog too," she whispered.

"Jasper!" The voice carried across the meadow and startled Emma. Instantly alert and focused, she stood and pushed Jasper towards the door. "Go, shoosh. Go home," she pleaded as she nudged him through the crack. "You can't stay here. Go!" Jasper, confused by her sudden change in mood, stood wavering with indecision, half in and half out of the doorway. "But I came here to help you," the big brown eyes seemed to say. "If I leave you now, you'll be sad again." But his new little friend seemed so intent on his leaving, that he finally gave in. With one last bright-eyed look that seemed to say, "I'll be back," he was off and heading for the house where Julia was just coming out to find him. As he rounded the side of the barn, she stopped and waited for him to come to her. "And just where have you been, you little rascal? Doing a little exploring of your own are you?" She scratched the big brown head and let her hand rest on his back as they walked back to the house.

Inside the barn, Emma sank to the floor once again and tried to decide what to do. There wasn't any way she could leave the barn today. It was already mid afternoon, and the

days were so short now she was
worried that she would have to
spend the night outside. She
decided that she would wait until
morning and then try to sneak into
the back of the man's' truck. Once
she was in town, she would have
the day to find shelter, and
hopefully some food. But for now,
for tonight, she would have to stay
here in the barn. She glanced
around, hoping she could find some
way to stay hidden just for this
night.

The men who had cut down the
stairs to the loft had put all her
things in one of the old crates that
were stacked in one corner of the
barn. As Emma started removing
them from the crate, she decided to

use the pile of boxes to create her new hiding place. She pushed them together to form a little cubby where she could just barely fit to lie down. She spread out her sleeping bag and blankets along the wall and stuffed her backpack underneath to serve as a pillow for sleeping and for something to lean against during the day. She knew that anyone coming into the barn could easily find her, but she was at least a little bit hidden if they didn't venture all the way into the barn. By the time she had that little task completed, she heard voices coming from the direction of the house. No longer able to see the house from her viewpoint on the second level, Emma had to rely on her ears to tell her if someone was heading towards the barn. She squeezed herself into the new little space she had created and stayed perfectly still. The voices she could hear belonged to the man and the little girl. They sounded as though they were heading towards the barn and Emma's heart started to race. She heard the man say, "It's coming down tomorrow. It's way too dangerous to leave standing, and I can't risk having you or anyone else getting hurt. I just want to check and make sure the door is closed tight so Jasper doesn't decide to wander in here." They were just on the other side of the barn now, and Emma thought for sure her time was up. Her breath caught when she heard the old door hinges rattle. Closing her eyes tight and clenching her hands together she chanted "Please don't let them see me, please don't let them see me" She was so deep in concentration that she didn't realize at first that they hadn't even tried to get in, but merely ensured that the door was secure. Their voices were now growing faint as the girl and man walked back towards the house. Emma released her breath and relaxed her taut muscles. Tomorrow she would make her move. Tomorrow she would sneak into the truck and get away into town.

"Did you have a nice visit with Henry?" Brinn asked Jasper as he greeted her with back end wagging

and pink tongue drooling. "I'll bet
he was glad to see you!"

"He certainly was," Julia added. "I
think it makes his whole day when
we drop by." Turning to Sam, she
added, "Henry says to dispose of
anything we don't want. Wendy
has already taken the things she
wanted and has given Henry all of
his personal things that he can
keep with him."

"Good to know," nodded Sam.
"Once we get that old barn torn
down and all the junk hauled away,
things will start looking a lot neater
around here. The construction
guys took the old stairs to the loft
down today just for safety
purposes, and they plan on being

here first thing in the morning to get started on the demolition."

"We'll have to keep a close eye on Little Miss Curious here, and her furry sidekick," Julia said, nodding towards Brinn and Jasper. "If we don't, the two of them will be right underfoot!"   They both laughed agreeably and watched as Brinn rolled a ball across the floor for Jasper.

Chapter 9

The next morning dawned crisp and clear. Emma was awake long before she heard any sounds coming from the house. She had already been out to her makeshift bathroom and was busily packing what she could into her backpack. She wanted to be sure that she made it to the truck before anybody woke up. She knew that once the big dog was let outside, he would make his way right back to her, and she couldn't let that happen. As she tucked her stuffed dog into the very last bit of space in her pack, she started to get butterflies in her stomach. It was scary to think of being out in the world all alone again. For the first time she truly realized how much comfort she had felt just being near this happy family, especially since the big scruffy dog had found her and become her friend. How good it had felt to hug him and snuggle up close. But Emma also knew that there was no place for her in this close-knit group. They already had a little girl, and a dog, and when Emma saw the lady on the porch the other day, she realized that soon they would be having another baby too. There was no way they would want some runaway ten year old who was probably already on everybody's bad list by now. She was certain that getting caught now would likely mean being returned to the group home instead of foster care so she wouldn't cause any other poor foster parents a lot of trouble. Nope, her only solution now was to sneak into the truck, get into town and find a new place to hide.

With one last look around at the place that had been her home for the past several days, Emma threw her knapsack over her shoulder and headed for the door. Before she even had a chance to pull on the old rusty handle, the sounds of loud machinery reached her ears. What was that? Emma was afraid to open the door and check on where and what was going on, but she was even more afraid of hiding inside where she was almost certain to be seen by anyone coming into the barn. In a moment of panic, she pulled the old door open just wide enough to stick her head out to see what was going on.

Her panic grew as she watched a large machine with a giant bucket on the front heading towards the barn. Behind it, another smaller machine followed, like two monsters engaged in a game of follow the leader. Both were heading directly towards the barn. Following close behind the two machines, were the two men that Emma had seen the other day at the barn, and the man from the house. They were talking loudly to be heard over the noise sand gesturing towards the barn. Next in line, but some distance back, the lady from the house was walking with the little girl and the big dog. She was holding tight to the girl's hand, and the dog was on a leash. They stayed back as the machines and the men reached their final destination. Obviously, they wanted to watch what was going on, but the lady was going to keep them out of harms' way. Scared almost into paralysis, Emma ducked back into the barn and closed the door. Instinctively, she ran back into the little cubby she had made. Her heart was racing, and tears were pouring down her face. She sank down onto the dirt floor hugging her knees and sobbing.

The machines were right outside the barn now, but Emma could no longer hear any voices. She had no idea what was going to happen next. All she wanted was for it all to be over.

Satisfied that everything was being done safely, Sam told the men to go ahead and get started. He walked back to where Julia and Brinn were watching from a safe distance. With her great sense of adventure, there was no way Brinn was going miss taking in this event. Sam put his arms around her shoulders and held her close while Julia stood next to them with Jasper on his leash.

Just as the first machine reached the side of the barn, Jasper broke free and headed straight for the barn. His sudden movement took

Julia completely by surprise and the leash slipped right through her fingers.

"Jasper, here!" both Sam and Julia yelled in unison. But the big furry dog was running frantically towards the big machine, barking as loud as he could. Julia and Sam stared in terror as he placed himself right in between the barn and the machine. The man in the driver's seat looked down in disbelief. Just one minute more, and the dog would have been crushed by the giant tracks of the machine. He idled the machine and leaned out the window. By this time, Sam was heading for the barn to retrieve Jasper. He grabbed the leash and tried to pull Jasper back and out of danger, but the big dog proved stronger than he expected. Jasper stood his ground barking and whining in front of the barn door. Sam continued to pull on the leash, eventually losing patience and yelling for the dog to get going.

Frightened by her dad's anger, and Jasper's unusual behavior, Brinn began to cry. All of a sudden, she was right there too, trying to hug Jasper and pleading with her dad to stop yelling at him. Both men were out of the machines now, just watching the weird turn of events, wondering if the dog had gone completely mad. Eventually, Sam was able to calm Brinn and grab the end of Jasper's leash. The crazed barking continued, however, mixed every so often with a long sad howl.

Having gotten to know Jasper so well since his rescue, Julia sensed there was a lot more going on here than anyone knew. She walked up to Jasper and took the leash from Sam. At first Sam was reluctant to let go. "Julia, you could get hurt if he decides to go crazy again. Let me get him back to the house." But Julia just shook her head.

"I know it sounds crazy, but I think he's trying to tell us something. I really think he has a problem with us tearing down the barn. Maybe this has triggered some memory from his past, or maybe there is something inside the barn that he's trying to protect. I have no idea what it could be, but I think we owe it to him to at least take him in and have a look around.”

“You better do something!” shouted the boss of the construction crew. “We’re not getting anything done as long as that mutt’s in the way. Time is money and you’re wasting a lot of it trying to figure out what some dumb mutt is thinking!”

Sam glared at him. “Well, it’s my money, so you just hang tight and don’t worry about it. And as for Jasper being some “dumb mutt”, you’d be smart not to let my wife or my little girl hear you say that. They wouldn’t waste any time showing you just how smart he can be!”

Turning back to Brinn and Julia, he said calmly, “Ok, let’s go see if we can find out just what Jasper is getting all worked up about!"

Emma sucked in a big breath and held back her tears when she heard the big old door creak slowly open.

Coming in out of the bright sunshine made it hard to see anything inside the dusty barn. Sam, Julia and Brinn stood just inside the door to let their eyes adjust to the darkness. Jasper didn't seem to suffer the same affliction, however, and he bolted across the open space and then stood barking. His masters followed him to a corner of the barn where several old crates were pushed together forming a little half wall. Jasper's bark turned to a whimper as they came closer.

"There must be something of Henry's in these old crates that he wants," Julia speculated. As she leaned over to peer into the top of the closest box, she sensed a very slight movement out of the corner of her eye. Thinking it might be a mouse or some other unfriendly barn creature, she jumped back. Grinning knowingly, Sam rounded the corner where there was a small opening in the group of boxes. He was prepared to watch a mouse scurry by, or even perhaps to chase a wandering raccoon back to the great outdoors. What he was not prepared for, was to see two big brown eyes looking back at him from under some very wild brown hair that fell in dirty strands around a tear streaked face. Before he even had a chance to speak, Jasper was pushing by him. The big old dog settled himself right beside the little girl and began licking away her tears. She smiled in spite of herself, and Sam looked on in wonder.

With one finger on his lips, he motioned silently for Julia to bring Brinn over. They huddled together, watching the dog and girl interact as though they had been friends forever. When Jasper at last looked up to see his people hovering nearby, he started running back and forth from one to the other as if making introductions. Mesmerized, Julia and Sam just stood there, but Brinn had no qualms about joining the party. She skipped right over to the spot where this newfound friend still crouched in fear. "Hi," she said. "My name is Brinn, and this is my dog Jasper. I think he likes you. He can be your dog too, if you want!" The sad brown eyes drifted back and forth from adults, to dog, to the little girl, unable to make direct contact. Suddenly recognition dawned, and Julia came forward and knelt down beside the tiny figure. "You're Emma, aren't you?" she asked softly. "It's okay, you don't have to be afraid. No one here is going to hurt you."

Emma nodded and the tears began to flow once again. "Please don't send me back. I can't go back." She was sobbing now, and Jasper was almost beside himself. He paced frantically back and forth between Sam and Emma, stopping long enough each time to lick her face, hoping to provide comfort and stop her tears. Julia held out her hand to Emma, speaking gently the whole time. "Let's get you inside and warmed up, and then we'll talk, okay? And don't worry, we're not sending you anywhere." Brinn smiled at Emma and took her other hand as they walked out of the barn. Sam turned to Julia and nodded towards the house.

"You guys head on home, I'll see to the work out here."   Before they had gone more than a few steps, Sam caught up with them to ask if Emma had anything else in the barn that she wanted. Emma raised her sad eyes to Sam's and shook her head. "Everything I brought with me is here in my bag," she said patting her backpack. Feeling his own eyes well up, Sam turned back towards the barn, while the others headed for the warmth of the house.

Brinn chattered away while they removed coats and boots and got Jasper settled down with a big chew bone. It was the only way they were going to stop him from licking the skin right off Emma's face. Julia led Emma into the big warm kitchen but didn't stop there. "I think a warm bath is the first thing on the agenda," she said as she led Emma up the stairs. "Then food, then talk, ok?" Emma had said very little up to this point, but the lady and the little girl were so friendly that she finally relaxed a little bit.

 "I haven't had a bath in a long time," she said quietly but with obvious longing.

"I know," said Julia, smiling. "And I think lots of smelly bubbles are called for too!" She filled the tub and watched Emma's eyes light up with anticipation. "You take just as long as you need, and here are some clean clothes for you to put on. They're from a bag of hand me downs that a friend gave me for Brinn. They may not be a perfect fit, but they'll do for now." With that she closed the door and left Emma alone to enjoy the first pleasant thing that had happened to her in a long time.

Outside the hum and buzz of machinery told Julia that the barn demolition was back underway. She checked to make sure Jasper and Brinn were still safe and sound in the kitchen. She was amused to see Brinn sitting beside Jasper as her chewed away, telling him what a good dog he was for saving Emma.

"You are a real hero," she whispered into his ear. Brinn somehow felt that it was necessary to speak right into Jasper's ear when she had something important to say. That was exactly what she had done that very first time she spoke after a year of silence. Julia felt tears sting her eyes as she remembered that sweet sweet voice whispering "My doggie. My doggie for keeps," in Jasper's ear. Since that day, Brinn had chattered nonstop to her new loyal and loving friend. Brinn looked up, sensing Julia watching her, and smiled.

Julia bent down and gave her daughter a huge hug. "You are awesome," she said. "And so is your furry friend, there. You guys were great with Emma."

"Is she going to live with us?" Brinn asked expectantly as though it should be just that simple.

"I don't know what's going to happen, honey" Julia said. "We have to talk to Emma first and then figure out what to do."

"Well I hope she can live with us," Brinn insisted. "Then Jasper could be her dog too." Julia smiled and brushed the hair that had escaped from Brinn's ponytail out of her eyes, letting the conversation drop.

After a while Julia headed back upstairs and tapped on the bathroom door. "Everything okay in there?" she called. She was answered by the door opening and a fresh clean face smiling back at her. The straggly brown hair was clean, and all traces of grit and grime were gone. Julia was amazed at the transformation. Standing in front of her was one of the cutest little girls she had ever seen. The big brown eyes were now sparkling and alert. Deep dimples appeared in each cheek when she smiled. Her upturned nose suggested just a bit of the determination and spunk that had probably helped her survive whatever tragedies life had obviously thrown her way. It took Julia a minute to find her voice. "Well don't you look good!" she finally said.

"The bath was awesome," Emma said. "Thanks."

"No thanks, necessary. Now let's get you downstairs and get some food into you." They walked silently together into the kitchen where Brinn and Jasper were still waiting. Brinn jumped up and ran over to

Emma. Jasper was right on her heels and in that moment, Emma felt more welcome than she had in a very long time.

"Hi," she said simply, smiling at Brinn and giving Jasper a rub. They sat together at the table while Julia made a hearty breakfast of bacon, eggs, potatoes, toast and muffins.

Sam walked through the door just as they were about to sit down. "Smelled the bacon all the way out to the barn," he laughed as he pulled up a chair beside the girls. "Well now," he said. "Look at these pretty ladies at my kitchen table!" Brinn giggled, and Emma smiled, making eye contact with Sam for the very first time. He too, was taken aback by the girl's transformation. He looked at Julia with raised brows and she nodded, understanding exactly what he was thinking.

They ate in silence for a while, and then suddenly Emma spoke. Overwhelmed by their acceptance and patience, she just couldn't help herself. All the fear and worry and loneliness of the past few days came pouring out like a bucket overflowing. Working backwards through the tragic events of the past six years, she told them all about running away from the Lindstrom's, and the foster home before that. She told them what she could remember about her parents being in the accident, and their cabin, and

Tucker and how all she thought she wanted was to get back home and live where she remembered being happy.

Although she was able to tell her story without crying, both Julia and Sam were struggling to keep control of their emotions. No strangers to traumatized children, they listened with genuine care and compassion. When Emma was finished, Brinn was first to break the silence.

"My Mom died too," she said with a matter of factness that seemed far beyond her years. "But now Julia is my Mom and we have Jasper and we live here in Jasper's old house and you can live here too if you want." Ever the optimist, Brinn summed it all up in one easy sentence. Emma couldn't help but laugh.

"I would love to live here, too," she said. "But I don't think it would be quite that easy!" She looked again to Sam and Julia. "Do I have to go back to the Lindstrom's? I really didn't like it there." Sam and Julia looked at each other for a long moment and then Sam spoke.

"We will have to call Family Services and let them know that you're here, and that you're okay. If you like, we'll also ask if you can stay with us for a few days."

"I'd like that a lot," Emma said quietly.

"Good, then all that's settled for now. I'll call a friend of mine who works for the county and find out where we go from here. For now, though, let's have a look at what's left of the old barn!" They all headed out to the back porch where they could see what was happening without getting in the way. There was already very little left of the original structure. A big pile of wood now filled the old foundation. In a while, two large dump trucks were to arrive and all the rubble would be hauled away. They watched the machines for a while longer, then Brinn asked if she and Emma could go up to the spare bedroom to play. Most of Brinn's toys had been parked there after the move until the family room could be organized. They were concentrating on getting the nursery finished first so the smell of paint would be long gone before the baby arrived. Julia told them to go ahead, but to stay out of the nursery where cans of paint were sitting on the floor between coats.

While the girls were busy playing upstairs, Sam made the call to his friend Declan Moore, a social worker who often came to the high school where Sam taught Phys Ed. Declan was great with troubled kids and Sam valued his professional opinion. He hoped that Declan would be able to help them keep Emma from being thrown right back into the system. He and Julia had immediately agreed it would be good for Emma if she could stay with them for a while until she was a little more stable emotionally.

After hearing the whole story, Declan agreed to talk to the people in charge and do his best to have Emma assigned to them as a temporary foster home. He explained that a visit from family services would likely come first, which would also include separate interviews with each family member as well as Emma herself. A report would then be filed, and a meeting held to approve the placement.   If all of that went well, Emma would be theirs until a new, long term foster home could be found. He told them not to worry, that it all seemed pretty cut and dried, and that the ruling should go in their favor. Sam thanked him for his help and went to tell Julia what to expect. They decided not to say anything to Emma until they had received at least a preliminary response from family services.

Emma, Brinn and Jasper stuck together like glue for the rest of the day. Emma was super patient and accommodating with Brinn's request to play Candy Land for the fourth time. Then they went out and threw a stick for Jasper until he collapsed on the porch, his sides heaving and his huge pink tongue dripping enormous puddles of drool. Julia brought chocolate milk and cookies out to the porch while they rested in the late afternoon sunshine. Julia's heart warmed at the sounds of their chatter, and a gentle little flutter in her belly told her that someone else was also enjoying the sound. The baby was becoming more and more active, and Julia couldn't wait for him or her to be with them. What a family they would be!

As the sun settled behind the trees, Julia called to the girls to come inside. Sam built a fire in the living room and girls and dog stretched out to soak up its warmth. Emma, exhausted from the events of the day, dozed off with her head resting on Jasper's back, while Brinn pretended to read one of her favorite books to her captive furry audience.

Chapter 10

The call came from family services early the following morning. A pleasant young lady by the name of Susan, asked if she might pay a visit to them that afternoon. She explained that, since Emma had been on the run for some time, it was important that they see her soon to confirm her health and well being. Sam told her that she was fine, but also that he understood their concern and that they were welcome to come to the farm any time. An appointment was set for 3 in the afternoon of that day.

Emma paced around the house, unable to relax after Sam told her about the pending visit. He tried to reassure her that they were only coming to make sure that she was okay, and that they weren't going to take her away.

"My friend has put in a good word for us", he told a worried Emma. "You're going to be able to stay here for a little while at least." With those words of encouragement, Emma seemed to relax a bit.

'Thanks," she said simply. "I really like it here."

Sam smiled and gave her a hug. "And we like having you here."

In spite of their best intentions, by 3 o'clock everyone was on pins and needles. Jasper had once again been confined to the mud room with another chew bone, and Emma and Brinn sat playing cards quietly in the living room, without any of their previous joking and bantering. Sam paced the floor, although he had no idea why, while Julia tried to remain calm. The sound of the doorbell made them all jump, and Jasper gave a half-hearted bark, not wanting to interrupt his meal. Sam opened the door and introduced himself and the others. Susan Kellerman was friendly and professional as she spoke to Emma, obviously assessing her emotional and physical condition as they carried on a light conversation. With introductions and formalities out of the way, Susan asked if she could speak with Emma privately for a bit. Sam, Julia and Brinn left them alone and went to sit at the kitchen table. In just a few minutes,

Susan poked her head into the kitchen and asked if she could now speak with Sam and Julia. Brinn was sent back to the living room to join Emma.

"Well," Susan began. "I must say, that is some brave little girl. She has been through a lot and yet she seems perfectly calm and collected right now. I think we owe a lot of that to you guys. I understand you'd like to apply for temporary placement?"

A look passed between Sam and Julia of total understanding. Julia nodded and Sam did the talking. "Actually," he said, maintaining eye contact with Julia as he spoke. "We'd like to apply to be Emma's long-term placement." When Julia smiled, he turned his eyes to Susan.

Susan looked from Sam to Julia and smiled. "I see," she said. "I think that you would be fine candidates for foster parents. I'll file my report with my highest recommendations, and we'll see what happens! We should have an answer with the week. In the meantime, I can see that Emma is in the best of care." She rose and extended a hand to first Julia and then Sam. "Thank you. It was a pleasure meeting you. I'll just pop back into the living room and say goodbye to Emma. I'll let you folks fill her in on what's happening."

Sam and Julia decided only to tell Emma that she would be staying with them for a while. They didn't want to mention the application for permanent placement in case it didn't work out. They told her not to worry, and that they would do their very best to make sure that she was happy. Emma was accepting of the news, happy that she would be staying here for a little while at least. She was tired of hiding, tired of being alone, tired of having no one to love her. If these few days were all the happiness she would have, then she was going to enjoy them. She hugged each of them in turn, saving the biggest hug of all for Jasper. Like Brinn, she bent down and whispered right into his floppy ear. "Thanks for finding me, Jasper, and thanks for bringing me home. At least for a while, you can

be my dog too." Jasper responded
with a big wet kiss right on her
cheek. Everyone laughed and
headed back to their places by the
fire.

Chapter 11

In the days that followed, the new little family grew even closer. Emma relaxed and her wonderful personality was permitted to shine through. Brinn blossomed even more with the attention of an instant older sister, and Julia and Sam enjoyed every minute with their "girls." They joked often that the baby better be a boy so that Sam wasn't so outnumbered, but it was all in good fun. Boy or girl, their only real wish was for a safe delivery and a healthy baby. Sam continued with the nursery and the girls went shopping together for baby clothes and accessories. Being busy made the time pass faster and Emma, especially was glad for that. As happy and relaxed as she was with Sam and Julia, the anxiety about finding a new foster placement was always there. She realized she was holding her breath every time the phone rang.

When the weekend rolled around with still no word, Julia suggested that Sam take the girls into town for lunch and a movie. Julia wanted to finish up some final paperwork before she went on maternity leave and needed some peace and quiet to get it done quickly. Sam agreed, and the girls were delighted. They ran upstairs to get ready with Jasper right on their heels. He didn't know what was going on, but he knew it must be good. The unfortunate thing he hadn't yet realized, was that he was likely going to be left at home. Waiting in the truck for more than three hours was hard on his joints now that he was getting older. He was always stiff after such trips, especially when the weather was cold. And besides, Sam really liked knowing that Jasper was home with Julia whenever she was there alone. Truth be told, the feeling was quite mutual. Julia liked the comfort and security of his big furry presence. Not that there was any need for a watchdog, or protector, but it was just nice to know he was there.

Now, with the girls and Sam gone, Julia found the house almost too quiet. She did have work that she wanted to get done, but the sound of Jasper snoring blissfully at her feet made her start to feel drowsy too. Instead of heading for the office, she sank down into the comfy living room sofa, drawing her knees up under her and resting her head on one of the overstuffed cushions. Before long she had drifted off. She was deep in a dream about summertime at the beach, where warm water was lapping around her feet and the sun was warm on her face.

Suddenly Jasper's incessant barking startled her awake. She opened her eyes slowly and realized that maybe the part of the dream about water had come from the puddle of water that had soaked her right through as she slept. A searing pain across her mid section brought her fully awake and aware of what was happening. When the pain subsided, she shuffled to the kitchen to find her cell phone. Jasper stayed right by her side, whimpering now, satisfied that his barking had raised the necessary alarms.

Julia hit Sam's number on speed dial and prayed that he hadn't yet turned his phone off for the show. Thankfully, he answered on the second ring. "Hi, what's up? Miss us already?"

"I sure do," said Julia. "And if you don't turn around and come home right now, Jasper may need to deliver this baby!"

There was a second of silence and then a shout. "We're on our way. Should I call the doctor? Are you sure you're ok? Should we call an ambulance?"

"I'm fine. My water broke and I think contractions are starting. They aren't serious yet, so we should be okay. Just hurry, Ok? But drive safe."

"Be there in fifteen," Sam said abruptly and disconnected. He flipped the phone closed and rejoined the girls who had gone ahead to get in line to buy their tickets. "Show's gonna have to wait, ladies" he grinned. "Looks like we're having a baby today!"

Brinn jumped up and down, clapping her hands and grinning

from ear to ear. Emma turned a worried face to Sam. "Isn't it too early?"

"It is, but Dr. Jameson said there was good chance Julia would deliver early. It's complicated to explain, but nothing we weren't prepared for. And nothing for you to worry about. Now let's get home!"

Jasper was right at the door to greet them when they got home. He jumped in circles, barking and whining, as much as to say, "I've done all I can. You take it from here." He led the way into the living room where Julia sat nervously waiting. She had changed her clothes and gathered up her hospital bag. Heddi James, an old friend from town was going to come over and stay with the girls while Sam was at the hospital. Julia turned to Emma and took both the girls' hands in hers.

"Do you think you can take care of Brinn and Jasper until Heddi gets here? It shouldn't be too long." Emma pulled herself up tall and stuck out the determined chin that had seen her through much more difficult challenges than this.

"I sure can. Don't you worry, we'll be just fine." She said proudly.

"I know you will," Julia said and gave her hands a squeeze. She and Sam headed off to attend the next big event in their lives. "We'll call you as soon as there is any news." She called from the car as they pulled away.

Heddi arrived at the door not a half hour later. She was a pleasant grandmotherly sort who started fussing over them right away. Brinn and Emma decided that since they had missed the movies that afternoon, that they would watch one of the movies from Brinn's collection. Heddi agreed to make them some popcorn and hot chocolate. She said that was her granddaughter's favorite movie snack, so Emma and Brinn didn't argue. Things in the movie were just getting interesting when the phone rang. Thinking it was going to be news of the baby, they both jumped up and raced for the phone.

Emma stopped short of picking it up, however, realizing with a jolt that it wasn't her place. This was Brinn's home, Brinn's family, and it was Brinn's new baby brother or sister who was arriving. Brinn sensed Emma's hesitation and understood. As much as she wanted to be the first one to hear the news, she motioned to Emma to pick up the phone, and was rewarded with the biggest grin she had ever seen on Emma's face. Emma picked up the handset and held it off to the side of her ear so Brinn could lean in and listen too. "Hello?" Emma said, expecting to hear Sam's voice. Instead, the soft voice of Susan Kellerman answered on the other end.

"Hello, is this Emma?"

"Yes, speaking," said Emma slowly. Her heart started pounding while she waited for the woman to say more.

"Is Julia or Sam there?" she asked.

"No. They're at the hospital. Julia is having the baby." Emma's voice now showed none of the excitement or anticipation that she had been feeling just two minutes ago. Suddenly she was scared, and all she could think about was not being a part of this family anymore.

"Oh, I see, "said Susan. "Well, I guess it's a night for good news all around, then. I'm calling to let you know that Sam and Julia have been approved as your permanent foster placement. You'll be living with them from now on. I hope this makes you happy, Emma."

For a few minutes Emma couldn't speak. Then tears began to flow down her cheeks even though she was grinning that great big grin again. Finally, she realized Susan was still waiting on the line.

 "Thank you. Thank you," was all she could think to say. Through the phone she could hear Susan laughing softly.

"You're welcome, Emma. Can you please ask Sam to call me when he has a moment? There's no big rush. We have paperwork to fill out, but it can wait. Tell him congratulations too okay?"

"I will," said Emma hanging up the phone. She and Brinn hugged and danced in circles, chanting and laughing and crying all at the same time. Jasper ran around them equally caught up in the excitement. They were making so much noise that they almost didn't hear the phone when it rang a second time. This time they picked it up together and leaned in to get the news they had been waiting for.

"It's a girl!" Sam's voice bellowed. "You have a new baby sister!"

"It's a girl," the girls relayed to an already teary eyed Heddi. "We've got a new baby sister." They listened while Sam gave them some details about the baby's weight and hair, and Julia's health.

Then Brinn took the phone into her own hands and spoke directly into the mouthpiece.

"Dad, "she said seriously. "Emma has some good news too." She then passed the phone to Emma. Emma tried not to cry as she explained to Sam about the call from Susan Kellerman. She could hear the tears in Sam's voice when he told her how happy he was, and how happy Julia would be. He said he would be home as soon as Julia and the baby were settled for the night. "Good night, girls," he said. I'll be home soon."

The movie was abandoned as the two new sisters chattered about future plans for themselves and their new baby sister. They both hugged Jasper, who was by now completely exhausted by the day's events.

"Guess what, Jasper," said Brinn in a singsong voice. "You get to be Emma's dog and the new baby's dog too!"

Emma hugged Jasper even tighter. "Now you're my dog too," she whispered right into his ear. Jasper looked from one to the other knowing that something good was going on. His girls were happy, he was home, and all was right with the world.

The End

Thank you for purchasing this book. It is readers like you who make the writing process so worthwhile. I hope you will help others to find this book by leaving a review on the book's sales page at Amazon.com.